PROOF COPY

BECCA WHITHAM

LETTERS FROM SANTA

O LITTLE TOWN OF CHRISTMAS COLLECTION

BY BECCA WHITHAM

Merry Christmas!
Becca

ISBN:1519456875
ISBN-13:9781519456878

DEDICATION

For my family.

You will recognize your names and few inside family jokes..

1

Fort Wainwright, Alaska
September, 1962

"*W*hat did you say your name was?"

Violet Poplovich repeated herself, spelling her last name for good measure.

The young soldier behind the counter interrupted before she finished. "Any chance you're related to Milo Poplovich?"

"That's my father's name, but—"

"Sarge! Hey, Sarge! You're never going to uess who's standing here!"

Violet pressed the pillbox hat deeper into her hair. How did he know her father's name? And why was he gaping at her? She lowered her gloved hand, smoothing potential stray strands as she went, and cupped the rounded ends of her Jacqueline Kennedy inspired bob. Was something amiss? She glanced down to verify the powder blue suit was in good order. All buttons in place and skirt correct, but apprehension prickled up her arms.

A second soldier appeared in the small space behind the counter at the Paymaster's office. He was tall and wiry, the exact opposite of the first soldier. "Where's the fire, Freddy-boy?"

"This is Violet Poplovich," Freddy-boy announced with the same awe reserved for movie stars.

Sarge turned round eyes on her. "Poplovich?"

Violet looked between the two soldiers. Her shoulders lifted with tension. What on earth? She was a simple librarian, but they stared at her like Audrey Hepburn had walked into their office. Crazy! Calling upon her experience dealing with unruly children, Violet stretched to her full five feet, four inches and lifted her chin. "Yes, and I need to speak to someone about—"

"Get Captain Stevens on the horn."

"Excuse me, Sergeant"—Violet checked the man's name badge—"Duston. That's the third time I've been interrupted in the space of two minutes. I would appreciate the courtesy of allowing me to finish my sentence."

"Sorry, ma'am, it's just that Poploviches are a bit of a legend around here. We got ourselves a captain asking about your dad."

Her heart pinched tight. A legend? Someone who asked about her father? This was all wrong. She inhaled through her nose, and the stringent tang of antiseptic transported her back to the hospital emergency room beside her mother's blue skin and blood-soaked hair. Violet swallowed hard. A strangled groan escaped and her face heated. "I am nobody's legend, I assure you, but I do need to speak to someone about discontinuing my mother's survivor's benefits." She spoke the words in a rush. Eleven weeks after her mother's death, the wound scraped open every time she needed to handle estate matters.

Freddy-boy picked up the black phone handset and dialed. "Captain Stevens, please."

Violet gripped her purse tighter and waited for the phone conversation to unfold.

"Captain Stevens? This is Private Neill from the Paymaster's Office. You'll never guess who's standing in front of me this very moment." He looked at Violet and smiled like she was dessert. "No, sir, the daughter. Yes, sir. I will, sir." He hung up. "If you'll come with me, please, Miss Poplovich."

She followed him outside and into an adjacent building, working up the courage to ask where they were going and why.

They twisted and turned down a labyrinth of narrow hallways until she was too lost to find her way out. Private Neill opened a door. "Miss Poplovich, sir."

Her legs wouldn't move. Who was this man, and why would he be asking about her long-dead father? It made no sense. Her heart pounded worse than the day policemen came to the library and escorted her to the hospital.

The private tipped his head to one side. "Miss?"

Automatically responding to the command in his question, Violet stepped inside a small, windowless office that looked and smelled like a converted janitor's closet.

The phrase, "Tall, dark, and handsome" was coined for the man who stood when she entered the room. He could pass for James Garner's sibling, complete with the Maverick TV star's squared jaw and mischievous grin. "Miss Poplovich. I'm Alex Stevens."

Violet shook his extended hand, glad her gloves protected against direct contact.

He stared like her face needed to be memorized. "I can't believe I finally found you."

He'd been searching for *her*? But the other soldiers said… Oh, she was so confused. Violet sat before her legs gave out. She needed to get the conversation back to why she'd come. "I don't know who you think I am, Captain, but I'd like to get this matter cleared up and be on my way."

Her businesslike tone shifted his expression from delight to something defensive. He leaned against the desk with cool nonchalance. "What matter?"

"As I tried to tell the other two gentlemen, I'm here to inform the army to stop sending my mother her survivor benefit check."

He crossed his arms. "Your mother isn't getting survivor benefits."

Violet searched his face. Was he joking?

He stared back, his elevated brows and tilted head daring her to contradict him.

Of what?

"Don't be ridiculous." She snapped her purse open. It took three tries before her white gloves captured her mother's check to wave under Captain Stevens's nose. "See."

He took the check and studied it, a disturbing twinkle in his gray eyes. "That's from the First National Bank of North Pole."

"Which is precisely my problem." She snatched the check from him and stuffed it away, every movement stiff and jerking. Her pillbox hat slid forward, so she pressed it back into place. "After my mother died, I advised the Paymaster's Office down at Fort Lewis to cease her survivor benefits. Instead, they transferred them up here, I'm assuming because I told them I was moving from Tacoma, Washington, to the Fairbanks and North Pole area."

The Captain's lips twitched. So he was joking. What a cruel thing to do! Her fingers curled. She clicked her purse clasp shut and envisioned slapping the smile from his face. The situation wasn't funny. Any gentleman worthy of the name would console a grieving daughter, not laugh at her. But this handsome cad with his black hair and broad shoulders apparently thought himself above common decency.

Violet set her purse on the floor. "The gentleman at Fort Lewis said he'd forward the information through the appropriate channels. I realize mistakes can be made in an organization as large as the army, so I came today to clear things up. Instead, I'm getting a first-class run around, and I'm quite tired of it."

She pulled a hanky from her sleeve and dabbed at the corners of her eyes, pressing the cloth against her nose to block the cloying scent of Lysol.

His expression softened. "I'm sorry. In all the time I've been searching for you, it never occurred to me that you wouldn't know the story."

"Searching…for *me*?" She reached out to grip the desk and knocked his name plaque askew. When she straightened it, she saw the words *Military Intelligence* under his name. Her ears buzzed, and a weight settled on her chest.

He sucked in a breath and blew it out through rounded lips. "I don't know how else to say this, Miss Poplovich, so I'm just going to give it to you straight."

Violet pressed her right hand against her racing heart to keep it from pounding through her breastbone. She gripped the wooden arm rest with her left hand to keep from floating out of her own skin.

"My father was an officer in Combat Command B back in World War II. Your father was an enlisted man under his command. They both disappeared a month after the Battle of Bastogne. The army has listed them as deserters." He delivered the blow with the same passionless intonation as schoolchildren reciting spelling words.

The words garbled inside her head. She asked him to repeat it. Twice.

"Im-impossible." Violet choked the syllables into the air. Desperate to breathe fresh air, she grabbed her purse and stood. "My father died during the Battle of the Bulge."

Captain Stevens stepped in front of the door. "I'm sorry, Miss Poplovich, but everything I just told you can be verified by army records."

"Verified?" If what he said was true, her mother had lied. The floor slanted under her feet

"I've been looking for your father since I was eight, hoping to learn what actually happened the day my father disappeared. I've gone over it and over it, and the only explanation that makes sense is your father deserted and mine ran after him to bring him back."

"I don't...believe..." The room went gray. Violet heard *The Twilight Zone* TV show's theme song as if it came from another room. Pricks of white light danced along her peripheral vision and her bones turned to rubber. "I think I'm going to be sick."

She was swooped into strong arms just as her legs gave out.

*****

"Hey, Dr. Anderson." Alex held the door open for Miss Poplovich to enter the medical examination room. She'd recovered enough to insist she was fine to leave, but Alex wasn't letting her out of his sight. He convinced her to see a doctor before driving a car. How to keep track of her after the exam was still to be decided. "This"—he announced with the pomp it deserved—"is Violet Poplovich."

Brad stopped so fast his stethoscope bounced. "You're kidding me."

Alex grinned. "Miss Poplovich, this is my best friend and a decent doctor, Brad Anderson."

"Nice to meet you, Dr. Anderson." She extended her gloved hand.

7

Brad shook it. "You as well, Miss Poplovich. Won't you take a seat?" He turned to Alex. "You wait outside."

"Yes, sir." Alex's mocking salute didn't elicit the usual twinkle in Brad's eyes. Uh, oh. He was in for another lecture. He stepped into the hall to wait.

Ten minutes later, Brad came out of the exam room. "She's drinking some water. She'll be fine, but please tell me you didn't"—Brad squinted— "You did!" He tugged the stethoscope from around his neck. "I told you that straight-to-the-point, consequences-be-hanged style of yours would get you in trouble one day."

"Trouble? Are you kidding me?" Alex clapped his friend on the back. "This is an answer to prayer."

Brad pointed to a chair along the wall. "Sit. I'm going to lecture you, and I don't intend to be looking up your nose when I do it."

Alex sat. This one was going to be a doozey.

"I've never challenged you on your story because, frankly, I never thought you'd find Milo Poplovich or his family." Brad stuffed the stethoscope in his white coat pocket. "But you've got to face facts, my friend. Everything you think happened the day your dad went AWOL comes from your fierce determination to see him exonerated."

"Old news, buddy, but I'll tell you what *is* new." Alex leaned forward, the same excitement running through his veins as when Violet first showed him the check. "She thought her mom was getting survivor benefits because her dad died at the

8

Battle of the Bulge. She came here to cancel them, but when I said her mother never received survivor benefits, she showed me a cashier's check from the First National Bank of *North Pole*."

"You caused a young lady to feel ill, Alex."

"That's only twenty minutes from here."

"Do you have any remorse?"

"The money *has* to be from her dad. I think he's using a cashier's check sent from the bank so he doesn't have to give his name and address, but I think she"—Alex tilted his head toward the exam room door—"moved up here to find him."

Brad held up his index finger. "Hold it right there. I'm going to pass over your glaring lack of compassion for Miss Poplovich for the moment. This is exactly what I mean about wanting to see your father exonerated. You've conveniently ignored the fact that she came here of her own volition to end her mother's survivor benefits. That's honorable, not deceitful. How long ago did her mother pass away?"

"I don't know." The admission caught Alex in the stomach. "I didn't ask."

"Of course you didn't." Brad rolled his eyes. "Just like it would never cross your mind to think *your* father might be the one sending the check."

"What?" Alex jerked back. His head smacked against the wall.

"You pride yourself on straight to the point, well how's this? What if, rather than chasing after a deserter, your dad was the deserter, and Poplovich chased after him? What if your dad is sending those checks because he feels guilty about getting one of his soldiers killed? Do you feel that? How all the air just left the room and you can't catch a breath? *That's* how you made Miss Poplovich feel with your patented I'm-going-to-give-it-to-you-straight style. So you will go in there,"—Brad pointed at the exam room door—"apologize, and do whatever else is necessary to ease her distress, or I'll tear you limb from limb. *Kapish?"*

Alex crossed his arms. "Is there a nice way to say, 'Your father's a deserter,'? If so, why didn't the army brief the officers they sent to my home when I was eight?"

Seventeen years had passed, and Alex still heard his mother's scream. He'd never stop hearing it. Like an invisible hand reached down her throat and ripped out her soul.

The scream drove him.

It drove him to Bob Calvin's Grocery when he was ten for spoiled produce to put on the table. It drove him to study until his eyes blurred to get a college scholarship. It drove him into the army where he could chase down leads to prove his father's innocence.

Because he didn't know how else to make the scream stop.

In those seventeen years, nothing he'd done ever brought him as close as Violet Poplovich walking into his office fifteen minutes ago. Was it any wonder he wanted to skip past what she should already know to the part where they found the truth?

Brad leaned down, blue eyes blazing. "Nonetheless, you will apologize for causing the lady distress."

Alex nodded. His mother would tan his hide if she found out he'd been so ungentlemanly to a lady. He walked into the exam room and regarded Violet Poplovich, this time as a woman who *might* be ignorant of her father's desertion.

As Brad left, he mouthed, "Limb from limb," so only Alex saw.

"I'm very sorry, Miss Poplovich." The words sounded hollow.

She sipped her water, shoulders sloped and hat askew, tilting her head farther and farther back to drain every drop. After crushing the paper cup, she tossed it in the garbage can. "I need to go."

Alex clawed his thighs. Every nerve sizzled with the desire to lock her in a cell and make her talk. To get some satisfaction, some reward, after nearly two decades of fruitless searching. However, if he was ever going to get the truth from her, she needed to trust him. Something she was far from doing at this point.

"Tell me what you remember." Alex leaned against the door. It wasn't like he was keeping her from leaving. She hadn't gotten down from the exam table. "Please."

She pulled hairpins from the edges of her little blue hat, straightened it, and pinned it back in place. For a long moment, she sat still and silent, her eyes downcast. "Why?"

He swallowed down a measure of pride. "Because I'd like us to find the truth together.

Wouldn't you like to know if your father is still alive?"

She lifted her head and looked directly at him. Her eyes were the color of molasses, and he felt himself sinking into them. He held his breath while she considered him. Would she see he meant her no harm? That his earlier callousness stemmed from a need to follow every lead to its conclusion, regardless of the consequences? To her or to him?

She licked her lips. "What have you found out so far?"

He didn't want to admit how little he knew, but he owed her that much. "Most of it is speculation." He hated how she brightened. Her hope canceled his, and his was too precious after so many desolate years. "After the Battle of Bastogne, what was left of Combat Command B took a month-long rest to refit for the final plunge into Germany. On 20 February 1945, they attacked the Saar-Moselle Triangle and, within forty-eight hours, had advanced eighty-five miles to the Saar River. Two days before that victory, our fathers disappeared. Both are listed as deserters."

She nodded slowly. "And you think my father deserted but not yours."

Yes, but saying it again served no good purpose. "After I joined the army, I looked into every record that was open to me. They're sloppy, as you can imagine, with all the chaos of war added to multiple variations of what happened whenever more than two people are questioned about an event. Especially when they're questioned months afterward. It's a longshot to find out anything more, but whenever I'm posted to a new place, I check in every six months or so with the Paymaster's Office there and at any post within driving distance to see if they have any news of Milo Poplovich. I was in to see Sergeant Duston and Private Neill last week, as it happens."

"Why would they get news of my father?"

"Because, if he didn't desert, the first place he'd go was to claim a paycheck." Alex didn't bother to draw the obvious conclusion that, since no paycheck had been claimed, either her father was dead or a deserter. For seventeen years, the chances that Milo Poplovich was dead far outweighed the chance he'd survived.

Except a dead man didn't send cashier's checks to his wife.

Violet rubbed two fingers against her bottom lip, her eyes fixed on him. After what seemed like five minutes, she took a deep breath and dropped her hand to her lap. "I was five when my father died." Her words were airy, like she was having trouble catching her breath. "I remember the two officers who came to tell my mother. They were tall and serious with lots of colored ribbons pinned to their chests. We were living with my *Baba* at the time."

"Your Baba?"

She looked at him like she'd forgotten he was in the room. "My grandmother. It's Yugoslavian for 'old woman,' but we used it as a term of endearment."

He'd written to the grandmother, but the letter had come back with a hand-written note that the

13

addressee was deceased. He'd written every relative from Fresno, California, to Canton, Ohio, and come up empty. "Go on."

Her gaze lifted, seemed soft and faraway. "We moved very shortly after to Tacoma, Washington. I cried and cried, but Mom wouldn't move us back home. We didn't know anyone in Tacoma, didn't have family. She didn't even have a job."

Alex shifted his balance from one leg to the other. Either Mrs. Poplovich had been trying to hide from the consequences of being a deserter's wife or went someplace where her husband could more easily send checks without detection.

"I don't remember how long it took before Mom got her janitorial job, but it seemed like I spent a year sitting in offices while she asked for work." A small smile lifted the corners of Violet's lips. "Then she became a janitor for the public libraries. She worked nights and took me with her. While she swept and scrubbed, I picked out book after book to read to her. Of course, they were only picture books, but I made up stories, and she'd laugh and ask for another. I loved it so much. I think it's why I became a librarian."

Alex was drawn into her story, his assumption of her guilt fading with each spoken memory. His tight fingers relaxed.

"We'd come home from the library, she'd make breakfast and teach me letters so I could read stories instead of invent them, then we'd go to sleep. We had nothing and everything, and I was happy. When I started first grade, she got a job with the public schools. That's when I first remember being embarrassed about my clothes and our apartment." Her expression tightened, like something she remembered didn't make sense.

"What?" Alex whispered, hoping not to break the spell she'd woven, his heart beating loud.

She stared directly at him. "On my seventh birthday, I came home from school and opened the refrigerator. I was looking for some bread and margarine, but there was"—she shook her head, a look of disbelief narrowing her brown eyes— "butter, *real* butter, and eggs and fruit and real milk and cream. I was sure I was in the wrong house. I screamed for my mother, half afraid I might have the wrong mom, too. She danced me around the table, said our money troubles were over because my father's survivor benefit check had finally come through, and then she gave me a..." She jerked straight, twisted her wrist, and pushed back the edge of her sleeve to see her watch. "I have to go!"

2

$\mathcal{A}$lex walked Violet to her blue Chevy, an inward debate raging over whether to follow her to wherever she was going in such a hurry.

Take all the time you need, his commanding officer had said when Alex phoned to say that Miss Poplovich had shown up. Alex doubted that included leaving post to follow a woman.

But, if he didn't, he might lose his last chance to find out what happened the day his father disappeared. In four months, he would transfer to Fort Riley in Kansas. The orders were in process. Violet Poplovich was here. Now. And about to get away.

Violet's blue Chevy backed up and pulled away. Before rational thought kicked in, Alex sprinted for his car. His heart pounded as hard as his feet, pounded harder when he followed Violet past the gate guards. It threatened to pound from his chest when she headed south on Richardson Highway toward the town of North Pole.

Alex kept at least three cars between his and hers. Twenty minutes later, she parked in front of a small, white building with a painted "Santa Clause House" sign across the top. Beneath it was a picture of Santa and advertisements for souvenirs, drugs, and fountain drinks.

He waited for her to go inside before sneaking in. The general store included a post office in back, where Violet conversed with a woman bouncing a toddler on her hip.

"Can I help you with something?" a masculine voice asked.

Keeping his eyes on Violet, Alex answered, "No thanks, just looking." He edged closer, picking up cans of peaches or wool socks as if he were interested, until he overheard "letter drive" and "thank you for chairing it, Miss Poplovich." He grinned, his heart lifting with hope and humor. Flyers requesting volunteers for the annual *Letters from Santa* drive were posted on every bulletin board at Fort Wainwright. And Miss Poplovich was leading it. At least ten soldiers would be on her list by tomorrow morning.

His name would be first.

Because Alex intended to find every possible way to be around Miss Violet Poplovich. If she truly believed her father was dead, or if Milo didn't appear to reunite with her, time would tell.

If not…

*****

After her meeting with Nellie Miller at the Santa Clause House, Violet drove straight to the bank. For the hundredth time since meeting Captain Alex Stevens, she played her seventh birthday like a movie inside her head, everything as she'd described until she got to her mother's explanation. "Your father…your father sent…well, the army sent a survivor benefit check, so I went a little crazy buying groceries."

Was it a trick of time or the seeds of doubt planted by Captain Stevens adding the stutter to her mother's words? After so many years, did she even remember them correctly?

Her birthday present that year—the thing that reminded her of the meeting with Mrs. Miller—had been a letter from Santa. When she went back to school the following day and told her friends, they'd laughed at her. Santa didn't send birthday cards, they'd said. At the time, she thought it was like her shabby clothes, something only poor children understood.

More scenes played through Violet's memory like commercials advertising the captain's version of the past. When cleaning out her mom's tiny closet after her death, Violet found a shoebox full of deposit slips—starting at fifteen dollars and, through the years, reaching a hundred—bound together with rubber bands. Mom always said their house was too small for sentiment, so why save what amounted to trash?

Violet also found the letters from Santa sent every Christmas, Easter, and birthday. Not the ones

Violet had written *to* Santa, just the ones that had come back. Letters which kept her believing in red-suited benevolence far longer than other children.

Stranger still, the deposit slips and letters were stored together inside a hat box buried under a pile of shoes on the closet floor.

Was her father alive? Had he—disguised as Santa—sent checks and letters?

What kind of man did such a thing? To desert the battlefield was one thing, but to desert his family? It made her furious and sad and hopeful all at the same time. She didn't want a deserter for a father. She wanted the hero her mother spoke of with such tender love.

But if he was alive…

She longed to meet him, to be wrapped in his arms rather than imagine how it must feel. To touch his face rather than his picture. To hear his voice rather than the one she'd made up during her imagined conversations with him.

Violet pulled into the parking lot in front of The First National Bank of North Pole. It didn't live up to its grandiose name. The cement block building was compact and showed signs of having endured harsh winters.

What kind of fool believed the army used such an insignificant institution to issue survivor benefit checks?

Violet rubbed the raw ache running down the sides of her neck. Her kind of fool, that's what, because nothing else fit the stories her mom told through the years.

She clicked open her purse and withdrew the sinister check. The paper was pale blue, like the light filtering through the yellow leaves outside her car. She ran gloved fingertips over her mother's name. OLGA POPLOVICH.

Did you lie to me, Mom?

Everything inside rebelled at the thought. Violet flung the check onto the passenger side, tore off both gloves to pile on top of it, and gave into the sobs. They started under her ribcage, hard and constricting, then ripped through her lungs. Large, unstoppable tears streamed down her face. She wiped and wiped, but they kept coming, tiny flecks and streaks from her mascara and eyeliner turning her fingers black.

The pain was worse than when she'd laid her mother's body in the ground. She'd grieved all the tomorrows they'd never share, the memories they wouldn't make together. This pain—with its jagged edges of truth that answered too many nagging questions—robbed Violet of their yesterdays, too.

Gray-stained tears soaked into Violet's top. She grabbed her hanky and dabbed it against her chest, but the blue linen was ruined.

She wasn't ready. If her entire life was going to be shattered, she needed time to prepare.

The bank and whatever answers it held would have to wait.

*****

The three weeks of Alaska's brief fall came and went while Violet carted around the awful check.

Every night when she emptied her purse, it mocked her as a coward, and every night when she tucked it away again, she promised to deal with it tomorrow.

Except she didn't want to deal with it *at all*.

The thing Violet wanted more than anything was a whole family, a mom *and* a dad with their children making memories around Thanksgiving tables and Christmas trees, at birthday parties and piano recitals, during Easter egg hunts and Independence Day parades. Growing up, there'd been plenty of kids who lost dads in the war, plenty of others whose parents divorced, but safety didn't come in numbers. Sympathy didn't carve turkeys or wrap presents. Patriotism didn't lift you on its shoulders to better view marching bands and floats, not even when your father was a war hero.

Take that away, and what was left? A cowardly father and a lying mother. Which would feel like they'd died all over again. Except worse, because she'd be responsible for killing them.

Besides, she was too busy planning the *Letters from Santa* kick-off at the George C. Thomas Library. Built in 1909, it had once been a house but had served as a library for twenty years. The years had taken their toll. The floor slanted in some places and had sunken spots in others, the roof looked ready to collapse, and there were only three fire extinguishers for what amounted to a fire trap. It overlooked the Chena River, so evacuation plans included jumping into the glacier fed water, if worse came to worst.

On the last Tuesday of September, Violet readied the basement room where thirty-two volunteers would answer children's letters to Santa. She decorated with red and green paper chains, set up a stereo to play Christmas albums, and laid out plates of home baked gingersnaps to put everyone in a festive mood. Since she was supplying the food herself, she had to choose between cookies and hot apple cider because she couldn't afford both.

She was on the library's veranda porch welcoming volunteers and pointing them toward the basement meeting room when a truck full of soldiers unloaded in the parking lot, one of them the insufferable Captain Stevens.

Violet rushed inside and ducked behind the checkout desk. Was it a coincidence? He *was* in military intelligence. Could they spy on civilians and find out where they worked?

Nonsense.

She'd told him she was a librarian, and there was only one library in the entire area. She simply *had* to keep her imagination under control.

"What are you doing down there?" Julie Crites, one of the other librarians, dumped a pile of books on the check-out desk.

Violet fell sideways, her hip bouncing against the hardwood floor. "Don't scare me like that," she whispered and rubbed her injury.

Julie adjusted her horn-rimmed glasses with two fingers. "Sorry."

Struggling against her red skirt and tulle petticoat, Violet wiggled back to a kneeling position. "If you must know, I'm hiding."

"From whom?" Julie swiveled her head to scan the library.

Julie's composure multiplied Violet's embarrassment. "The volunteers."

A look of confusion tightened Julie's face. "I thought you *wanted* to head up the letter drive?"

"Doesn't mean I have to like everything about it."

"Well, don't let Mrs. Longley find you, and don't hide too long. You need to be done before we close in"—she checked her watch—"ninety-three minutes." Julie picked up a different stack of books and strode toward the non-fiction shelves.

Violet grabbed her purse from where it rested on the floor and snatched out the check she'd tried to ignore since meeting the captain three-and-a-half weeks ago. If he asked what she'd done about it, she needed to answer she'd taken care of it. Two rips later, she stuffed the pieces back in her purse and swiped her hands to remove trace evidence.

There. She'd taken care of it.

Before replacing her purse, she powdered her forehead and refreshed her lipstick. Too bad she'd worn flats instead of her highest heels. Violet stood and brushed dust from her blouse. She'd chosen the red and white outfit to color coordinate with the Christmas decorations. Her fellow librarians had thought it clever. Would the captain think her childish?

Why did she care what he thought?

Picking at stray pieces of lint all the way, Violet trudged downstairs. She clapped her hands to call everyone to order. "Thank you for coming." Good. That sounded just like she'd rehearsed in her bathroom mirror. "As you probably know, thousands of children write Santa every year, addressing their letters to the North Pole. Ten years ago, when the city of North Pole incorporated, letters began arriving to their post office located inside Santa Clause House. The owners, Con and Nellie Miller, decided to write back. Every year, more letters arrive, and the need for people to answer grows." She inhaled, half sure she'd delivered her entire speech in one breath.

Captain Stevens's presence felt like a splinter that could be ignored as long as she didn't rub it the wrong way.

Violet turned so he was invisible. It didn't help. "At your seat are approximately twenty letters from children and enough stationary to write a one or two page response to each. If you need more paper or your pen runs dry, please let me know. I've also provided envelopes without postage. That's in case you need to rewrite an address. We don't want to waste a four cent stamp."

A few chuckles and a "Certainly not!" echoed through the room.

"Speaking of stamps, at one end of the refreshment table are some decorated coffee cans." Violet walked to the table and held one up. The construction paper felt slippery in her hands, so she set it down quickly. "If you would, please take them to your work place or church to collect donations to cover the mailing costs. The Millers would appreciate it. In the center of the table are some mimeographed copies of sample letters. Feel free to use them or not as needed. Any questions?"

Three hands lifted, none of them belonging to the captain. Grateful for small blessings, Violet answered the questions, and then everyone settled in to write. She walked around the room helping as needed.

Her reprieve with the captain was short-lived. The instant his hand went up, her stomach went down. She finished spelling *reindeer* and forced her feet to the opposite side of the pine table. "Yes, Captain Stevens?"

"I can't decipher this word." His long finger pointed at childish scribble.

Violet leaned closer for a better look. The subtle tang of citrus and cedarwood filled her nostrils, like all the best parts of summer and fall rolled into one. She closed her eyes and breathed it in. Aftershave was her weakness, and this one reminded her of being swept into his strong arms.

"Miss Poplovich?"

Her eyes shot open. Focused on the word. Which started with a *C* and had what looked like an *a* in the middle. "Wow. That's quite a mess, isn't it?"

An older woman three seats down said, "Maybe I can help. I teach second grade." It took her five seconds. "Chatty Cathy."

"What's a Chatty Cathy?"

Every female head swiveled to stare at the captain. For a long time.

"A talking doll." Violet moved to help a soldier on the opposite side of the table, disgusted with the leering women. Yes, the man was handsome, but it wasn't like he was Rock Hudson. Of course,

Captain Stevens wrapped his not-quite-movie-star good looks in a uniform. To some, the combination was as heady as aftershave.

Those women hadn't spent ten minutes with the man being interrogated like a criminal.

Well, not exactly an interrogation, but it had *felt* like one.

For the next hour, Violet worked hard to give him the same encouragement she doled out to the others. Every moment she expected him to ask about the check. Every moment he didn't, she wondered how much longer he'd make her wait. She was exhausted by the time people started putting on coats. She picked up piles of envelopes and leftover stationery feeling like she'd escaped the executioner's block.

"Miss Poplovich?"

Chop! "Yes, Captain."

"Will we be meeting again next week?"

Violet chased a rolling pen that slipped from her nerveless fingers. "Every week through the first Tuesday in December."

He inclined his head in a modern-day bow. "Until next week."

She was so disconcerted by those three little words, she didn't see the large envelope he'd left on his chair until after he was gone. The seal in the top left corner shouted its contents—her father's army records.

Violet hid it underneath the pile of envelopes and mimeographed sample letters, but the yellow color peeked through like a tiger stalking its prey.

She read it, of course—like he'd known she would—while sitting at her kitchen table with nothing but a napkin basket for company. As she suspected, it proved Alex Stevens told the truth. Her father deserted, and her mother lied by calling him a war hero.

An odd tranquility settled over her spirit. A distance between facts and how she should feel about them. Like she'd become the narrator of her own story.

In that uncanny calm, she even admired Alex Stevens for being such a clever nemesis.

As she prepared for bed, she slipped into storyteller mode. "What the villain didn't know"— she angled her toothbrush like a microphone—"was that Violet snuck over to the door just in time to hear the good doctor's theory about the evil captain's father sending those mysterious checks out of guilt."

Violet continued her narration while removing her make-up with cold cream and setting her hair with pink rollers. By the time she was finished, the story had morphed into a fairy tale where Violet was united with her father who was so wealthy, he'd paid *The Tacoma News Tribune* to print a special HELP WANTED section advertising the North Pole librarian position and made sure it was delivered to Violet's door. He also paid to stage his wife's death. The story ended with a tearful reunion and the three of them escaping to Yugoslavia, where they lived happily ever after.

When Violet crawled into bed and turned out the light, the minor problems with her fairy tale magnified ten-fold. She fell into a troubled sleep and dreamed a tiger imprisoned her in candy cane bars while elves made Chatty Cathy dolls and Santa tossed letters into the air while laughing like a villain. *Mwah, ha, ha!*

The following morning, Violet drove to the bank with shaking hands and a stomach full of gravel. She showed the taped-together check to the manager. "I realize you probably can't tell me anything about who paid for this, but whoever it is needs to know that—" She stopped to suck down air. The remaining explanation lodged under her tongue, refusing to budge.

She didn't want to do this. She wanted to preserve the lie she'd grown up with where her mother was a paragon of virtue, the checks were army-issued survivor benefits, and her father was a war hero. It wasn't true. The records she'd read last night confirmed it, but to compound her father's desertion with confirmation he'd also abandoned his family…?

"Yes?" Light bounced off the man's shiny head.

"I'm sorry to bother you." Violet stumbled over the chair in her haste to leave. She ran to the door.

"Miss! Your keys!"

Violet grabbed the push bar and froze. If she didn't get this over with, she'd be back and have to face it all over again. She turned around and waited for the lumbering bank manager to get from his desk to the door. When the keys fell into her hand, she gripped the man's pudgy fingers and leaned close. "If you know who sent the check, please tell him Olga Poplovich is dead."

Did she imagine it, or did his face register shock?

"I'm her daughter." She let go of his fingers and stepped back until she was halfway out the door. "I work at Thomas Memorial Library."

3

*T*he last Saturday of September dawned unusually fine. Unwilling to waste such a glorious day, Alex packed his tackle box and fishing pole onto his motorcycle and headed to Chena Lakes. The leaves were already off the trees, but snow hadn't yet fallen. It usually came a week into October and harkened the quick decent into days with minimal light.

He spent eight hours in a rented boat, caught three fish, cooked two of them for lunch, and gave the third one away to strangers at the park. A perfect day, and one that made him regret his time at Fort Wainwright was coming to an end. In a few more weeks, though, he'd be glad he was heading to the lower forty-eight by January.

As long as he unraveled the mystery of Milo Poplovich's daughter first.

He'd thought about different ways to convince someone at the First National Bank of North Pole to tell him who was sending the cashier's checks. Each option either ended in failure, because it was none of his business, or him lying. He also couldn't use his Military Intelligence connections to dig into either Olga or Violet Poplovich. They were civilians. He'd already dug up everything he could on Milo Poplovich. To dig further was a waste of time. Besides, using army resources on what was a personal manhunt was as improper as lying to get a bank employee to reveal a customer's identity.

Violet was the key.

On his way home, he drove past the library. Her car was in the parking lot. There was no electrical plug hanging out her front grill. What was she waiting for? She'd been in Alaska for at least a month, and winterizing her car should have been her first priority. Was it possible she didn't know she needed an engine block heater to keep her oil from freezing during the harsh sub-zero temperatures?

Alex leaned into the turn and parked his motorcycle near her blue Chevy. He checked to be sure he hadn't missed a cord, noted her balding tires, and marched into the library. If she didn't have a plan for winterizing her car already, she'd have one before he left the building. A single woman unprepared for dangerous weather was a disaster waiting to happen.

Violet was in the basement, where the volunteers had written letters, but now the room was crowded with children sitting on the floor and

31

most of the parents standing along the windowless walls. Violet sat in a chair at the far end holding a large book with full-page pictures, the smile on her face as bright as sunshine.

He remembered how she loved telling her mother stories so much she became a librarian. A story she told him with a pinched expression that dulled the radiance currently lighting her face.

Guilt bowed his head.

He'd put that tense look on her face—with his straight talk that Brad warned would lead to trouble. Only by seeing the glow now, did Alex comprehend how much he'd hurt her that day.

A little boy squirmed free and ran to Violet. She scooped him into her lap with one hand without breaking her narration. Leaning down, she whispered the next part of the story like it was a secret she and the child were sharing. Her voice carried through the room, so no one missed a word of Babar's adventure. The boy's mother picked her way through the children to take her son back. Violet gave the woman a sweet smile and turned the page.

Alex leaned against the stairwell as enthralled with the story as the children. Violet was a taking little thing. Not pretty, exactly, but quite charming in her way. She loved children—and they her— which was a plus. If a man was looking for a wife. Which he wasn't.

She looked around the room, and their eyes met. All the joy drained from her face, and she stuttered to a stop.

Parents turned to see what had caused her reaction.

Chagrined by their curiosity and disconcerted by Violet's stricken countenance, Alex gave a quick wave. "Sorry to disturb, folks. Go on, Miss Poplovich."

Violet blushed bright pink. "Right. Where was I?" She flipped the page and started to read.

"You skipped a part Miss Violet." This from a blond girl with red hair bows.

"Skipped?" Violet turned a page ahead.

"No, go back!"

The command earned a sharp, "Be patient," from the boy's mother.

Looking like she wanted the floor to swallow her whole, Violet went back two pages and started to read, her words lifeless and face wooden.

The children fidgeted, no longer fascinated by Babar's antics. A few annoyed glances came Alex's way.

Should he go?

No. Not until he found out whether she already had an appointment to winterize her car.

When the story ended, the children pleaded for another one, a better one. Violet froze, her eyes flitted to him before dropping.

The mother whose son had run away glared at Alex. "Not today, children."

He felt like a thief caught with one foot out the window, but he needed to finish the task at hand. He stepped into the room and off to one side so people could exit.

Violet stayed and chatted with various women. Judging from the sharp looks coming his way, they were offering to shield Violet from his unwanted company. Whatever she said reassured the ladies enough that they gathered their children and purses. But if looks could kill, Alex died at least ten times before the room emptied.

"What can I do for you, Captain Stevens?" Violet clutched *Babar the Little Elephant* to her breast like armor.

"I actually came to see if I could do something for you."

He'd never seen someone frown with their entire body. "For *me*?"

"Is that so hard to believe?"

Her tilted head and loose jaw practically screamed, *"Yes!"*

Alex pressed his lips together to keep from mounting a defense of his actions. From her perspective, he'd made her ill and followed her to work twice. No wonder she mistrusted him.

"I was driving by the library and noticed your car." He kept his tone light and friendly. "I didn't see a cord coming out. Since you've never been through an Alaskan winter, I wasn't sure if you knew about winterizing your car."

Her shoulders dropped a fraction. "I don't know what that means."

Alex explained the need for engine block heaters, sub-zero anti-freeze, and traction tires. "The snow will be here soon, so you'll want to hurry."

"How much will all of that cost?"

The way she asked told Alex more about her finances than she probably realized. "New tires will run you fifty to sixty dollars."

"A piece?" She paled and looked ready to faint.

"No, for all four." This information didn't appear to relieve her. Alex disliked adding to her burden, but facts were facts. "An auto shop will install the engine heater for around twenty-five or thirty dollars, or you can buy one for about five and I can install it for you."

*****

Violet wilted onto the nearest chair. Eighty-some dollars was more than her monthly rent! Friends had warned her Alaska prices would eat every penny of the eye-popping starting wage advertised for a librarian. She'd ignored them. Her mother's memory haunted every corner of Tacoma, and coming home to the little house they'd shared had become pure torture. Where better to start over than North Pole, the place responsible for sending children letters from Santa and making Christmas magical?

After spending an incredible amount of money driving through Canada, she'd discovered Fairbanks and North Pole apartments cost two times what she paid for a whole house in Tacoma. Added to that were exorbitant heating costs. The realtor suggested she rent a "dry" cabin until she built up enough savings for an apartment. Thrilled with the price, she signed a three month lease figuring she could manage without running water for ninety days and survive with the cord of wood stacked beside the front door. Now it looked like she'd be there all winter long.

"Do you have a good coat and winter boots?"

If Alex Stevens asked her one more question, she was going to scream. "I brought some from Washington."

"I doubt they're insulated enough."

Did he have to be so unfeeling? Her distress couldn't be more obvious, but instead of offering assurance, he piled more problems on her plate. What a monster!

"You'll also need gloves, a hat, wool socks, and a thick scarf to cover your nose. How much can you afford?"

Violet set the book on the floor before she threw it at his head. He made her feel foolish and needy when she wanted to appear smart and independent. She dropped her chin and touched the ribbon in her hair as she bit color into her lips. Pasting on a smile, she lifted her head. "I'll manage."

"Look, Violet, I know you think I'm a monster for—"

"I would never say such a thing!"

"—being so blunt but, if there's an elephant in the room, it's still going to take up the same amount of space if you paint it pink." His shrug said, *"You can't argue with logic."*

In spite of herself, Violet laughed. "And you've wasted a gallon of paint."

"Exactly." He stepped closer and sat on the floor. The action made him less intimidating, more likable. "I realize you have reason to mistrust my motives after our first meeting, but I swear to you I only want to help. Alaska winters are like nothing you've ever experienced. If you're not prepared, they can kill you."

"But I have until January or February before the brutal weather kicks in."

His frown was three parts denial and one part incredulity. "Who told you that?"

"I just assumed..." Violet rubbed her forehead. "What am I going to do?"

"Like I said, I can install the engine block heater. That'll save you about thirty bucks."

She didn't want help from him, not in any way, shape, or form. On the other hand, thirty dollars was a lot of money. If only one of the churches she'd visited had been friendlier. She could've asked a pastor to recommend someone in the congregation to help. Maybe she could ask Julie, or the head librarian, Mrs. Longley. Perhaps Mr. Longley could...

Wait!

What if Alex's offer to help was a ploy to hang around in case her father showed up?

Would he?

The question felt like a betrayal. Her father wasn't alive. He hadn't deserted. She wouldn't believe it. But just in case...

She lurched to her feet, narrowly avoiding tripping over Alex with a quick sidestep. "No time like the present."

Could she ask for a few hours off after a month's employment? She couldn't afford to lose her job. Violet headed for the stairs.

"Do you want this book?"

She'd forgotten. "Please bring it with you." She climbed the stairs without a backward glance.

Julie was behind the checkout desk. Only a handful of patrons browsed the shelves. When Violet explained her need, Julie's eyes grew wide. "You haven't winterized your car?"

"I didn't know I had to." Violet took *Babar the Little Elephant* from Alex's hand and placed it on the desk.

Julie put it with the pile waiting to be re-shelved. "I'm so sorry. I should have mentioned it. I've lived here forever. I guess I forget not everybody understands our harsh winters or how suddenly they arrive." She eyed the captain. "Is he helping you?"

At Violet's nod, Julie winked. "Oh, yes, you definitely need to take care of that today. I'll be happy to cover for you."

Violet turned to see a smug grin on the captain's lips. She grabbed her purse and coat. "Let's go."

Alex held the doors open for her, forcing her close enough to smell his intoxicating cologne. "I'd offer to take my car, but I brought my motorcycle today."

The man was worried about winter weather, and he drove a *motorcycle*? Were it not for the horrified look on Julie's face two minutes before,

Violet might have turned around and marched back into the library. "I'll follow you."

"No sense wasting gas." He put his hand out, palm up. "I can drive."

Violet clutched her purse tighter. "Captain Stevens, I've known you a grand total of two hours. I don't intend to turn my car over to you or even allow you inside it. Waste of gas or not, I will follow you."

He stopped in his tracks.

She kept walking, inserted her key in the lock, and opened the door. After setting her purse on the bench seat, Violet straightened and looked at Alex.

He was still standing in the middle of the parking lot looking like she'd stolen his lollypop. "What do you think I intend to do with your car—other than make sure it's safe for you to drive?"

"Probably nothing, but I would feel safer in my own vehicle. Alone."

Would he renege on his offer to help? If so, she'd know what kind of man he was.

4

$\mathscr{A}$lex mentally counted to ten. How dare she impugn his integrity? After he offered to *help* her.

Then he remembered how he'd treated her at their first meeting.

"You're right, Miss Poplovich. I'm sorry I presumed too much." It came out stiff, but at least it got past his throat. "If I get through a light and you don't, I'll pull over and wait for you."

Her shoulders relaxed. "Thank you."

They got to the auto parts store without mishap. He offered to pay for the engine block heater as an apology for being presumptuous, but she wouldn't hear of it.

Independent little thing.

She led him back to her house, if you could call it that, and fixed dinner while he installed the heater. Her log cabin was no bigger than a one-car garage with an outhouse in back. Despite her immaculate cleaning, it still felt dingy. Alex wanted to haul her to the nearest apartment complex and pay whatever it cost to get her settled, but remembering her reaction to a five dollar engine block kept him quiet.

It seemed nonsensical that she'd not ride in a car with him, but she'd show him where she lived.

Contrary woman.

She served meatloaf with mashed potatoes, gravy, and a side of green beans with tall glasses of milk. Nothing fancy, but substantial and filling. They ate outside on the little porch and talked about Alaskan winters—how the cold froze your eyelashes and stung your nose—and when to view the Aurora Borealis. She asked about his work. He couldn't tell her much, but he made sure she knew where the nearest fallout shelter was. Not that any Soviet nuclear missiles would penetrate this deep into Alaska, but it would make her feel better should some of the threats he was tracking at work come to fruition.

The sun started to set, casting a pinkish glow over the austere cabin. She brought out a plate of gingersnaps and set it on the crate acting as a table. "They're leftover from Tuesday night's letter writing." She bit into one and licked crumbs from her lips.

"I enjoyed that." He snapped a cookie in half and dipped it into his milk. "Since you've just arrived in the area, how did you know about the annual letter writing campaign?"

She stopped chewing, a look of panic in her eyes. "Why do you want to know?"

Her reaction raised the hair on the back of his neck, but he kept a casual look on his face. Something about letters made her want to hide. Why? He placed the milk-soaked cookie into his mouth and chewed. "Idle curiosity."

To emphasize his complete—and fake—lack of interest in her answer, he ate the other half of his cookie without looking at her.

She picked up her milk and swallowed a gulp. "I can't decide what to do with you, Captain Stevens."

Good to know he wasn't the only one. He gave her his best smile. "Alex. Please."

Eyeing him like a roach crossing her cookie plate, she set down her milk glass. "What do you want from me?"

"Exactly what I told you the first time we met. I'd like to figure out what happened to our fathers on the day they disappeared."

"I don't believe you."

His hackles rose at the accusation. "Why not?"

She squinted. "Because you want to prove your father a paragon of virtue and mine a coward. You aren't after truth, you're after your version of it."

He opened his mouth to argue, then snapped it shut. Was he? Brad had accused him of the same thing, but… "Wait a minute. You were eavesdropping on my friend and me talking in the hall, weren't you?"

"Maybe." Both her tone of voice and crossed arms dared him to find fault.

He couldn't help but admire her spunk. "All right then, what do you say we call a truce? You share your information—including why the mere mention of letters makes you defensive—and I'll share mine. We work together to unravel why two paragons of virtue suddenly deserted the battle on the verge of victory."

"And you'll give my father the same benefit of the doubt as you're giving yours?" Her arms crossed tighter over her chest.

He stuck out his right hand. "On my honor."

*****

Violet eyed Alex's hand. If she shook it, she was committed. Did she want to be? No, but the constant back and forth inside her mind was driving her batty. "Before I agree to this, I want to add one caveat."

His eyebrows lifted, but his hand remained outstretched.

"If we find the truth, I want us to agree on any action we take as a result."

He lowered his hand. "What do you mean?"

Violet rubbed her left elbow. "Let's say we discover your father was the deserter, and he's been living in Alaska for fifteen or so years. Wouldn't you want to hear his story before I notified the army?"

"His story?" Alex frowned like she was speaking a foreign language.

"Yes. Why he disappeared, where he went, what he's been doing…his story?"

He rested his forearms on his knees. "I don't see what difference it makes."

Violet stood and cleared dishes to put space between her and a man's thick head. Alex followed, bringing the rest of the dishes inside with him. The kitchen—the entire cabin—was too small. His presence filled every corner. Like the day in his office, Violet needed air, but she needed to make him understand even more. An inexplicable sense of destiny, or at least of unstoppable events put in motion, insisted time was running out.

For whom, she didn't know.

She reached under the cabinet for a plastic tub and scraped bits of food into it. Water was too precious to waste washing anything extra. "I think stories matter. They might not change what happened, but they add clarity and maybe even some justification. If your father were suffering from battle fatigue, wouldn't you want to know before he was turned over for prosecution?"

Alex leaned his hip against her counter. "What do you know about battle fatigue?"

"Until three weeks ago, I thought my father died in the Battle of the Bulge. I've read every account and suffered along with the men stuck in trench holes with freezing water up to their necks. I've cried over how their buddies to the left and right were shot and died agonizing deaths within earshot while those who survived were helpless. If half of what I read is true, it's amazing more men didn't run for their lives. Have you *ever* faced anything so terrifying, Alex?"

"No, but—"

"Then how can you sit in judgement of someone who did?"

He rubbed his chin, the *shush* of beard stubble against calloused fingers audible in the tiny space. "Look, Violet, I get it. Your compassion is admirable…enviable in some ways…but it doesn't change the facts. Soldiers who desert in the face of the enemy must answer for their actions. A tribunal will take into account battle fatigue before pronouncing judgment, but justice must be served."

"Maybe it already has." Violet swiveled to face him. "Think about the kind of life someone must have led to stay hidden this long. I've lived without running water for seven weeks, and I'm ready to scream. Compound that with no electricity, no oil heaters, no job, nothing but subsistence living in the harshest climate possible for more than fifteen years. Isn't that punishment enough?"

"And what of my mother?"

Violet recoiled like she'd been hit. "Your mother?"

A mocking smile tilted his lips. "I do have one, of course."

"That's not what I meant, and you know it." Violet stomped back outside and swiped crumbs off the crate.

Alex followed. He grabbed her hand, spilling crumbs on the porch, and pulled until she sat. He picked up his chair, set it opposite her, and sat down, still holding her left hand in his right. "I'm sorry, Violet. You seem to bring out the worst in me."

Except for the part that worries about me being safe in winter.

45

Violet blinked against the unwelcome thought. She wanted to despise Alex Stevens, but she found she couldn't. The reason why was a question for another day.

He took her other hand, pressing both of hers between his own. "My mother raised three boys on less than a janitor's salary. Unlike yours, mine never received checks from an unknown benefactor. She never moved where no one knew her husband deserted. She sold our family farm for less than she owed and moved us five miles into a two-bedroom, one bath rambler we shared with my grandparents. My brothers and I slept end-to-end like sardines in a double bed, while my mother slept on a folding lawn chair in the living room. When my grandfather died, we made due on housecleaning jobs and paper routes. You can imagine how many people wanted Mom inside their homes to clean when she was jeered in the streets, shunned at church, and spit on at the grocery store."

Violet pulled her hands away to wipe the tears that dripped down her cheeks. Her heart burned with sympathy. If Alex's sense of chivalry wouldn't let him pass by a stranger in need of an engine block heater, how much more must he ache for his mother and struggle against his helplessness?

He pulled a handkerchief from his pocket and handed it to her. "It's not as bad now. My grandmother died a few years ago, and all three boys have moved out, so a two-bedroom suits her just fine. She even has a job as a secretary. If my father is proved guilty, her life doesn't change. I can live with that. But if he's proved innocent, she not only gets survivor benefits but seventeen years of back payments and redemption in her community. That's what I'm fighting for, Violet. That's why I can't let this go. Do you understand?"

She nodded and blew her nose in the soft cotton. Then she went inside and brought out the letters from Santa she'd received since she was seven so he could read them and examine the envelopes. He looked them over without comment. There were no clues, nothing his trained eye could decipher beyond the obvious...

Someone was pretending to be Santa and, whoever he was, lived near enough to North Pole, Alaska, to use their post office.

There was nothing more to say. Alex thanked her for dinner. She said it was the least she could do in light of his work on her car. He promised to share new information. She nodded and promised to return his handkerchief after washing it.

If he noticed she said nothing about sharing information, he didn't say anything before he left.

The yard felt smaller without him. Colder, too. Violet picked up the letters and clutched them to her chest. She desperately wanted to believe Dr. Anderson's version that the checks and letters from Santa were sent by Alex's father, but the place reserved for a truth too sharp to soften with fairy tales knew better.

No man would send strangers money without also caring for his own family. Certainly not a man whose legacy was someone like Alex.

That left one choice.

Santa had to be her father. A man she didn't know, wasn't sure she even *wanted* to know, yet yearned to meet with every breath. If they found him or, more likely, if he came out of hiding to find her, she'd be responsible for sending her father to prison.

God, is there a happy ending in any of this?

5

$\mathcal{F}$or two weeks, Violet survived Tuesday's letter-writing nights. She and Alex managed friendly conversations before he settled in to write letters, but she was glad when he left. The less she saw of him, the more she could pretend her life wasn't on a collision course with heartbreak.

Snow fell and the temperatures dropped. The days were dark by five-thirty in the afternoon. Violet's rubber boots kept out the wet but not the cold, and her coat would soon be too thin. She went shopping, but the cheapest parka was seventy dollars, and the Salvation Army Thrift Store didn't have anything even close to her size. Besides, new tires were next on her list.

Violet found a home church on the second Sunday in October. Although the congregation was welcoming a new pastor, they didn't allow her to get lost in the crowd. Their hospitality spilled over her soul like a balm. The woman sitting one pew ahead even introduced Violet to the choir director, who was thrilled to hear she was a First Soprano. Violet agreed to come back for Wednesday night practice.

She showed up three days later and was organizing her music in a folder when Alex walked in. Had she really thought this church was an answer to prayer?

God, what are You thinking?

Violet turned her head to hide by engaging the woman on her right, but the thirty-something blond was staring in Alex's direction.

"What a catch." The woman turned her head another ten degrees, her blue eyes twinkling. "I'm Mrs. Jennifer Mauer. What's your name?"

"Miss Violet Poplovich."

"Well, Miss Violet, what do you think of our most eligible bachelor?"

"I hadn't noticed him." Violet looked at the chalkboard and pretended to double check her music against the order of rehearsal.

"He certainly noticed you." The laughter in her voice meant Mrs. Mauer wasn't fooled. "If Mr. Melhorn hadn't cornered him, I think he'd be over here talking to you. He was definitely looking your way."

The woman on Violet's left leaned forward. "I want to know what's happening with Cuba. President Kennedy said he was going to order a crackdown on the fourteenth. That was three days ago."

While Jennifer and the other woman descended into politics, Violet calculated how rude it would be to escape. Of all the churches in all of Fairbanks, he would walk into hers. Or she into his. Whichever. It was still a *Casablanca* moment.

Mr. Smith, the choir director, asked everyone to take their seats. He introduced Violet then promptly asked the pianist to begin warm up exercises. Grateful she'd not have to deal with Alex Stevens for the rest of the hour, she hadn't counted on him sitting two seats behind her, his rich baritone voice impossible to ignore.

Drat and double drat the man!

When practice was over, the group's friendliness became a trap rather than a blessing. Violet kept trying to get out the door, but everyone in the choir wanted to welcome her to their group or invite her to celebrate "Alaska Day" with them tomorrow. Fortunately, everyone also seemed to have a question or piece of advice for Alex. From Soviet trawlers horning in on Alaska's crab harvest to the Soviet Union sending nuclear warheads to Cuba to the East Germans refusing to allow an ambulance to help a man shot while trying to cross the Berlin Wall, people treated Alex Steven's like their personal insider to government secrets.

Violet escaped first. A light snow was falling, the flakes small and dry like powdered sugar. She pulled her coat tighter around her throat but was shivering by the time she reached her car.

"Violet! Hey, Violet!"

Triple drat the man!

Politeness turned her around. "Hello, Alex."

He picked his way across the parking lot, stepping where patches of snow provided some traction over a layer of ice. "Listen, I—hey, your teeth are chattering." He pulled off his coat and wrapped it around her shoulders.

Violet tried to wiggle out of the warmth before his spicy cologne weakened her knees, but his grip on the fabric was too tight. Figuring it was the fastest way to get rid of him, she stopped struggling. "Now you'll freeze."

"Not really. Look, I just wanted to say that you shouldn't stop coming to church here because of me. They're a great bunch of people, and I'll be gone in a few months anyway."

Something akin to disappointment flitted through her. "Where are you going?"

"Fort Riley, Kansas. In December or January, depending on my orders." His eyes flickered to her lips. "I'd better go. See you Sunday?"

She returned his coat, and he opened her car door for her. "See you Sunday."

That momentary look at her lips chased Violet all the way home and the following morning to the local pool.

One good thing about no running water in her cabin was that she'd started swimming again. The shower afterwards was hot if a little prickly on her skin from the water pressure. After toweling off, she dressed and put on some makeup. She set her hair in rollers, attached the drying cap to the air hose of her portable dryer, and wrestled the cap over the rollers. While she waited for her hair to dry, she read "To Kill a Mockingbird." She'd read it two years ago when it won the Pulitzer Prize, but with the news reporting James Meredith's every move at the University of Mississippi at Oxford, the topic of racial prejudice was fresh on her mind.

The adventures of Scout, however, couldn't keep Violet from thinking about Alex Stevens and his mother.

While she'd worked her way toward the choir room door last night, Violet overheard Mrs. Mauer ask where Alex had been on Sunday. His answer—sending a tape-recorded letter to his mother courtesy of the local USO—dropped another stone into Violet's already heavy heart.

She closed the novel and imagined what Alex had felt watching his mother be spit upon. Had *her* mom experienced something similar? Was that why she'd moved them from California? If she had, lying about the desertion made sense, because it protected her *and* Violet. Lying was wrong. Of course it was wrong, but it was understandable. More importantly, protecting them might have been the sole reason her mom lied.

Except those mysterious checks still needed to be explained.

Checks that put a buffer between her and the kind of poverty Alex experienced. It was easy to imagine Alex and his brothers faced the same ridicule and shunning as their mother while growing up.

No wonder he burned for justice.

Was knowing his story enough, though? If she were faced with her father—something she longed for and dreaded with every breath—could she turn him in? She sympathized with Alex, but she'd *lived* her childhood.

Violet lifted the dryer cap edge to see if her hair was dry. It wasn't, but she couldn't spend another moment alone with her thoughts. She removed the rollers and styled her hair using a wide headband. It made her appear sixteen, which almost convinced her to set the rollers and try again, but she didn't care what Alex Stevens thought of her.

Almost.

Not that he'd show up to the library on a Thursday.

But *maybe* he would.

If only she could stop thinking about the last piece of advice her mom gave for choosing a husband. "Watch how he treats his mother, because that's how he'll treat you in ten years." Alex cherished his mother, defended her, made her a priority. What would that feel like?

Heat spread from her heart to her arms, legs, and face. How had the man gone from her mortal enemy—well, sort of an enemy—to potential husband material?

*****

Alex scratched the back of his neck. He needed a haircut. And he needed to figure out what to do about Violet Poplovich.

He looked at the calendar. Monday, October 22. Tomorrow marked four weeks from the day she showed up with the cashier's check, the first major lead in finding out what happened to his father. It hadn't led to anything, and he was starting to lose hope again.

He couldn't follow Violet all the time. If she was meeting her father on the sly, she was a marvelous actress, because she seemed as innocent as a child. With all the spunk and curves a woman should have.

And every time they met, the urge to kiss her got stronger.

Brad Anderson opened the office door without knocking. "You got a minute?"

"Sure." Alex checked his watch. A few minutes after fifteen-hundred. "Two more hours before quitting time, buddy. What's up?"

"Have you heard?"

The hair on Alex's arms stood at attention. "About what?"

"President Kennedy is addressing the nation about missile sites discovered on Cuba."

"When?"

"Right now." Brad sat and leaned an elbow on the desk.

Alex swiveled in his chair and turned on the radio. President Kennedy's distinct voice filled the room. "The characteristics of these new missile sites indicate two distinct types of installations. Several of them include medium range ballistic missiles, capable of carrying a nuclear warhead for a distance of more than 1,000 nautical miles. Each of these missiles, in short, is capable of striking Washington, D. C., the Panama Canal, Cape Canaveral, Mexico City, or any other city in the southeastern part of the

United States, in Central America, or in the Caribbean area."

Brad mouthed, "Did you know?"

Alex shook his head. His intelligence gathering was limited to what Soviet ships and subs were doing in the Pacific.

"Additional sites"—the President's voice continued—"not yet completed appear to be designed for intermediate range ballistic missiles— capable of traveling more than twice as far and thus capable of striking most of the major cities in the Western Hemisphere, ranging as far north as Hudson Bay, Canada, and as far south as Lima, Peru. In addition, jet bombers, capable of carrying nuclear weapons, are now being uncrated and assembled in Cuba, while the necessary air bases are being prepared."

Brad's eyes got big. "Holy Smokes."

Alex nodded.

When the president got to the points of action, Alex pulled out a pad of paper and took notes.

1. U.S. Navy to blockade ship's cargo of offensive weapons; not denying necessities of life
2. Increased close surveillance of Cuba; armed forces to prepare for any eventualities
3. Any attack launched from Cuba against any nation in W. Hemisphere considered an attack by Soviets against U.S. requiring full retaliation

4. Guantanamo evacuated of dependents; military on standby alert basis
5. Call to invoke Articles 6 and 8 of the Rio Treaty
6. Call for emergency meeting of U.N. Security Council
7. Call on Khrushchev to abandon course of world domination, help end arms race

The president wrapped up his address. "My fellow citizens, let no one doubt that this is a difficult and dangerous effort on which we have set out. No one can foresee precisely what course it will take or what costs or casualties will be incurred. Many months of sacrifice and self-discipline lie ahead—months in which both our patience and our will will be tested, months in which many threats and denunciations will keep us aware of our dangers. But the greatest danger of all would be to do nothing.

"The path we have chosen for the present is full of hazards, as all paths are; but it is the one most consistent with our character and courage as a nation and our commitments around the world. The cost of freedom is always high, but Americans have always paid it. And one path we shall never choose, and that is the path of surrender or submission.

"Our goal is not the victory of might, but the vindication of right; not peace at the expense of freedom, but both peace and freedom, here in this hemisphere, and, we hope, around the world. God willing, that goal will be achieved.

"Thank you and good night."

The phone rang.

"Good afternoon, sir. Did you hear the speech?" Alex recognized the voice of his unit's First Sergeant.

"I did."

"Good. Base is conducting an inventory of all personnel and weapons. An accountability formation will be held in the ready room at seventeen-hundred."

"Anything else?" Alex held up a finger to tell Brad he'd relay the information in a moment.

"Yes, sir. Your change of station orders are on hold until further notice."

Alex swallowed hard. "On hold" meant it wasn't worth moving someone who was just going to end up in a war. "Got it. Thanks, Sarge." He hung up and relayed the information to Brad.

"Your affairs in order?"

The silent question was, *Are we still battle buddies? You'll look out for my family and I'll look out for yours?* "Yes. You?"

Brad nodded. "Let's pray it doesn't come to that. Okay, I'm off to get ready for the inspection."

They stood and shook hands. It was a little firmer and longer than usual.

At the door, Brad stopped. "Whatever happened with Miss Poplovich?"

Alex gave him a brief version, including Violet joining his church choir. "I told her not to stop coming on account of me, and she showed up for Sunday Service yesterday. I guess that means she can put up with me for a few more months." Either he'd be in Kansas or someplace much farther away.

"I'm glad you made things right." Brad swung the door open. "She seemed like a nice girl."

After he left, Alex sat at his desk trying to absorb the repercussions of the blockade against Cuba. The next few days would determine if a nuclear war broke out. Logic said no country would ever start what would end in total annihilation, but logic didn't always win.

Alex bowed his head and prayed for his president, his country, and—should it come to war—*Please, God, let me have what it takes to stand rather than run.*

How he wished he could protect his mother and brothers from what they just heard, let them hold on to their sense of security.

The irony struck him.

Faced with her husband's desertion, Violet's mother decided to protect her child. Violet had only been five years old when her father disappeared. Perhaps the plan was to tell her later, or maybe only if Milo Poplovich were caught. To give Violet a hero father rather than a criminal one. To shelter her from harsh reality until she was old enough to handle it.

Did he wish *his* mother had done the same?

Instead of herding her three sons around her the moment the officers showed up, what if she'd heard the news alone? Had the courage to leave home? Given them all a fresh start?

Not lie, just soften the truth.

He'd been eight, his brothers ten and six. Hadn't their age warranted some protection, even if they were boys?

Not that the past mattered. The real question was, in the face of a possible war, who needed the most protection now? His mother lived in the same house he'd grown up in. Still had many of the same neighbors, many of whom had gradually accepted her back into their circle of friends. Even if all three sons were drawn into a war, Mr. Calvin would take care of her. He had been ever since he started saving "past due" groceries to send home with Alex when he was ten. Alex doubted any of those items were ever past due, but he didn't doubt Mr. Calvin loved his mother. Someday, she'd accept one of his annual proposals. They'd started the day after Alex's father was declared legally dead and continued for the last ten years.

Between her three sons, Mr. Calvin, and Brad, she had five men to care for her. Surely one or more of them would survive, even if another war broke out.

On the other hand, who would take care of Violet Poplovich?

6

*V*iolet, along with the rest of the library patrons, listened to the presidential address on a portable transistor radio. As soon as it was over, she went to the lavatory and cupped her hands to sip cold water.

One sentence from the speech kept running through her mind. "No one can foresee precisely what course it will take or what costs or casualties will be incurred."

Casualties like Alex Stevens.

What would happen to his mother if he died? Or worse, what if, like her husband, her son disappeared without a trace? Could she live with the strain of not knowing?

Violet bent over the sink and sucked down air.

If merely imagining what it would be like to have Alex missing in action caused her lungs to stop, what must the reality be like?

When she returned to the check-out desk, Mrs. Longley pressed a hand against Violet's forehead. "You feel a bit warm. Do I need to send you home?"

"No. I'll be fine in a moment. The broadcast upset me."

Mrs. Longley looked around. "Why don't you take a little break to settle your nerves."

"Thank you. I think I will." After putting on a coat and rubber boots, Violet made a bee-line for her car.

She needed ice cream.

Lots of it.

Preferably chocolate.

The air was chilly but not bad enough she'd catch a cold. She picked her way across the parking lot and saw odd shapes in the snow around her car. A closer inspection revealed four new tires. Someone had rolled around on the icy ground to change them out for the old ones, which were stacked behind the bumper with a large plastic bag on top.

She opened it and found a long parka with a faux-fur lined hood. There was no note in the bag, but in the left front pocket she found an envelope. Heart hammering, she opened it and pulled out a Christmas card. Inside, under the printed greeting, was a hand-written note:

Dear Violet,
   Please accept this as an early Christmas present.

Love,Santa

Violet dropped the card into the bag and stuffed the parka on top. She checked the parking lot. Was her Santa watching now? She'd told the bank manager she worked here. Had her father come after all?

The signature didn't look quite the same as the ones on her childhood Christmas, Easter, and birthday cards, but it was twenty-four degrees outside. Perhaps the signature suffered from the cold.

An icy finger of fear traced her spine. What if this secret Santa wasn't her father? What if it was someone she didn't know? She'd heard news stories of women followed by crazy men. Frightened, she hurried back inside the warm library still carrying the bag.

Chocolate ice cream would have to wait.

Possible Santa options ran through her head. When Alex had tried to pay for the engine block heater, she'd refused. Would he attempt to get around future refusals by pretending to be Santa? It didn't seem like something he'd do, but how well did she really know him?

Keeping her head down, she rushed to the check-out desk and dropped the bag underneath it. She took off her coat, rolled it in a ball, and stuffed it inside the bag along with her purse. A girl set a stack of books on the desk. Violet stamped the due date in each while the girl signed her name on the check-out cards.

A steady stream of patrons kept her hands busy, but not busy enough to distract her mind.

Con Miller, the owner of Santa Claus House, was famous for playing Santa for area children. It was how his store got its name. He and his wife might have supplied the parka and changed her tires. She'd been to North Pole to deliver letters and donations a couple of times. They might have noticed her needs and decided to supply them. No doubt the Millers would be at the North Pole Elementary carnival next Saturday. The newspaper advertisement said the PTA was looking for help. She could volunteer and, while she was there, at least ask the Millers if they were responsible.

When her shift was over, Violet stopped by the community bulletin board and copied down contact information.

Tuesday night, neither Alex nor the rest of his soldiers showed up to write letters. The mood was somber. The school teacher who'd deciphered Alex's Chatty Cathy doll request broke down in tears when the letter she was addressing was to a child in Key West, Florida. "It's so close to Cuba."

Violet did her best to soothe the inconsolable woman, but there wasn't much to say. What if there was no Key West by Christmas? She ran upstairs to get a pamphlet from the Homefront Mobilization about how to stock a fall-out shelter and what to do in case of a nuclear attack. By the time she got back downstairs, conversation had moved to whether Colonel Witt should remain the Fairbanks Civil

Defense Director, or if he should be replaced by a man with higher moral standards. She stuffed the pamphlet in her pocket to read at home later.

Alex stopped by the library on Thursday. "I only have a moment, but I wanted to check in on you. How are you doing? Are you okay?"

"As well as can be expected." Violet gripped her hands behind her back. He looked so good, so strong, so much like a man she wanted to hold tight and never let go. She opened her mouth to tell him about the tires and parka, but he looked toward the door. Now wasn't the time. Besides, she didn't have any new information.

Not really.

"How about you?" She searched his face. Men were notorious for hiding their feelings. He looked frazzled but not panicked, and he didn't look like he was trying to hide something.

"I'm fine. Sorry we didn't make it Tuesday night. Things have been pretty hectic on post between this Cuban thing and getting ready to test the new Pershing Missile next month." He took a step back. "Listen, I really have to go, but you're sure you're okay?"

"I'm fine. How's your mother?"

He jerked upright, a look of surprise on his face. "My mother?"

"I assume you've called her, despite the astronomical long-distance charges."

Alex grinned. "She's fine. As per usual, she wouldn't let me talk for longer than three minutes. She keeps a stop-watch by the phone and hangs up at two minutes, fifty-eight seconds whether I'm done talking or not."

"Good." Violet waved her hands to shoo him out the door. "Go on, then. I'll see you on Sunday."

*****

To everyone's great relief, the Soviets turned their ships around on Friday without a single shot fired or missile launched. Saturday afternoon story time, the children were full of plans to go see Miss Margaret from *Romper Room* down at the Piggly Wiggly.

All was right in the world again.

Violet headed to North Pole later that night, a Red Velvet cake on the seat beside her, with a much lighter heart though still bothered by her mysterious Santa.

When she arrived at the carnival, the Millers greeted her with a warm hug. She asked if they knew where her new tires and parka came from. Their looks of surprise told her they hadn't given them to her before their words denied it. Although they did have a type of present for her.

"We'll be sending a Santa up to the library to thank your volunteers once we can get him pinned down on a date." Nellie Miller wiped a smear of chocolate from her thirteen-month old daughter's chin.

The same icy finger from the parking lot six days ago ran down her back. "Who?"

"His name's Dan." Con Miller took Violet's Red Velvet cake and started for the desert table. "Good man. He's the one who gave us the idea to

send letters from Santa to children on their
birthdays."

Violet stopped walking. "B-birthdays?"

"Yeah. And he seems to know you."

Her mouth went dry and she hurried to catch up
with Mr. Miller. "How?"

He waved at someone across the gym. "We
didn't have much time to talk, but it was something
about a cashier's check."

*****

Alex hung up his choir robe and tried to catch
Violet's eye. She was ignoring him.

Why?

She'd seemed fine when they chatted on
Thursday. What changed in three days?

With November right around the corner, the
church had begun their annual "Invite a Soldier for
Thanksgiving Dinner" campaign. He'd received
several offers after service ended, all declined
because Mrs. Mauer beat them to it at choir practice
a few days ago.

Had anyone invited Violet?

If not, he'd breach protocol and ask Mrs.
Mauer to include Violet. No one should be alone on
a holiday, particularly the first one after her
mother's death.

Violet disappeared while he was assuring
several men that the Cuban Missile Crisis was
indeed over and there was no evidence that the
Soviet trawlers invading Alaskan waters had been
spying instead of crabbing.

He declined three invitations to join various families for lunch saying he had other plans. Not that Violet knew she was part of them, but he was going to get some answers before the day was over. He drove to Violet's house and knocked on the door.

"What are you doing here?" Her eyes were rimmed in red.

"Can I come in?"

She looked away and shrugged.

Good enough. He stepped through the door and took off his coat. The pot belly stove put out heat and the scent of burning wood. "What's going on, Violet? And don't tell me nothing."

"It's not nothing, it's just…" She rubbed her hands together like she was distributing lotion. "I don't know what it is, so I'm not sure what to say."

He was about to say, *"How about the truth,"* when he noticed her table. Empty except for a napkin basket. It was the end of the month, so perhaps she didn't have any food in the house. "Can we talk about it over lunch? My treat."

Her mouth opened and closed. It was a remarkably kissable mouth.

The room got unbearably hot. Alex tugged his shirt collar. He needed to get out of her cozy little house, and she'd balk at anything too expensive. "LaRaine's Homestead has a two-dollar, fifty-cent spaghetti dinner. Would that be okay?"

She hunched her shoulders. "I don't think—"

His stomach rumbled.

Loudly.

When she started to giggle, Alex knew he'd won the battle. "C'mon. It's just spaghetti."

She nodded and reached for her coat.

He grabbed it quickly to assist her, glad to see she'd purchased something heavy and with a hood.

All the way to the restaurant, he kept up an innocuous flow of chatter—asking how she felt about John Steinbeck saying he didn't deserve the Nobel Prize and the proposal to use Old City Hall as a new library site. The conversation lasted until their spaghetti arrived.

"Why are you avoiding me, Violet?"

Her knife and fork clattered onto the plate. The stricken look in her eyes made him feel monstrous. "I'm not..." She looked down and pulled her shaky hands under the table. "No. That's not true. I *am* avoiding you."

"I won't bite. I promise." He scooped a large helping of steaming spaghetti into his mouth. "Shee"—he lisped around the noodles—"my mou' ish 'ull"

She laughed. "I know. It's nothing you've done."

The admission warmed him more than the food burning his tongue.

She raised her eyes to the ceiling, blew out a breath, and faced him. "A couple things have happened since we last talked about our fathers, and I don't know what to do about them."

While she told him about the parka with its Santa-signed Christmas card, the new tires on her car, and the mysterious Dan who knew about the cashier's check and was coming to the library dressed as Santa some Tuesday night to thank volunteers, Alex chewed on both his spaghetti and the information.

"What if this Dan person is actually…" Violet looked toward the window.

"One of our fathers?"

She shook her head. "It's not your father. Why would he take care of me and my mom and not you and your family? That wouldn't make sense."

When they'd met six weeks before, he would have felt an I-told-you-so triumph. Now, it felt like he'd eaten too much too quickly. "So you think it's your father?"

"Who else could it be?" Tears trickled down her pale cheeks. "All my life, I've looked up to him as a hero. I don't know what to do with this new father—this deserter. Nor can I silence the voice inside my head telling me not to trust him."

Alex swallowed down a bit of spaghetti threatening to come back up.

"Why did I tell the North Pole bank manager I worked at the library? What if I'm being followed by some kind of crazy person? I know I'm letting my imagination run wild, but I can't seem to help it."

A primitive urge to protect flooded Alex's entire body. He reached his hand across the table, palm up.

She placed her small hand in his and squeezed it tight.

Her trust, fragile as it was, filled him with an overpowering desire to wrap her in his arms and never let go.

Violet wiped her cheeks with her free hand. "I started off by painting this elephant pink and, as you cautioned, it didn't help. So now I've gone the complete opposite way and am seeing boogey men under every rock."

He pushed his plate aside and put his other hand on top of hers. "Don't worry, Violet. We'll get through this together."

She squeezed his hand. "The voice in my head says that you, of all people, understand what it's like to suddenly find your father has feet of clay."

He nodded and let go of her hand before he couldn't. "I've never stopped hero-worshipping my father. Instead, I've created a scenario whereby my father is completely innocent of any wrong. Now who's painting the elephant pink?"

Friends had tried to tell him the same thing for years, but the lesson hadn't been learned until he'd put himself in Violet's shoes and recognized the pain his version caused this woman he was coming to care for.

Violet looked at him—really looked at him—for a long time. When her shoulders relaxed and her eyes softened, he knew he'd passed an important test. "Thank you for that, Alex. I appreciate it more than you know."

The waitress stopped at their table. "Is everything okay?"

Alex watched Violet's reaction closely. "Any chance we can get a doggy bag?"

"Not on an all-you-can-eat night. Sorry." The waitress started to take the plates away.

Violet put up a hand. "No. Don't take it just yet."

"Yes, ma'am." A crash turned the waitress's head. "If you'll excuse me."

After Violet swallowed down a couple bites, she pushed the plate aside. "I'm sorry, but…" She made a face.

Alex stood and held out his hand. "Let's go. I know a great place for cinnamon rolls. We can get a couple and either eat there or take them back to your place, whichever you prefer."

She brightened. "That sounds perfect."

They ended up getting two cinnamon rolls to go and taking them to Violet's house. While Alex stoked the wood stove, Violet made hot chocolate. Alex informed her that, whether she liked it or not, he'd be chopping firewood to fill her insufficient wood pile.

She didn't argue, just forked a gooey bite of cinnamon roll into her mouth and sighed. "Perfect."

Frosting clung to her bottom lip. Alex reached across the table to wipe it with his thumb. Her skin was warm and soft. She inhaled at his touch. From the way she held her breath and leaned to follow the trace of his finger, he thought she'd welcome the kiss he ached to give her.

But it was too soon, and not a good idea when they were alone in her house with nothing but a crackling fire to chaperone. Next time—and there would be a next time—he'd take her somewhere where the food was good and the goodnight kiss was even better.

Emboldened by her reaction, Alex laid out his plan for protecting her from the unknown Santa. "First of all, you're not leaving the library without an escort."

"It's not practical for you to come every night."

Pleased beyond reason she thought about seeing him that often, he hid a smirk behind his mug of hot chocolate. "Then get one of the other librarians or a patron to walk you to your car on the nights I'm not there."

"Yes, sir." She added a salute for good measure.

Her saucy grin had him thinking about kissing again. "Second, I think you should ask Con Miller for a little more information on this Dan fellow. Find out his full name, where he works, how long he's been in the area, that sort of thing. I can go with you, if you like."

She shook her head. "I don't think that's a good idea. If he is my father, questions like that might send him into hiding. And if he's watching from afar and sees me with a crew-cut, soldier boy, we'll never see hide nor hair of him."

"Right but—"

Wait"—she held up a hand like she'd done with the waitress earlier—"hear me out. I've thought a great deal about your mother and what finding the truth might mean for her. I want to make it safe for him to talk to me. Since it appears he's willing to come to the library dressed as Santa, I say we let him come whenever he's ready."

That was the second time she'd thought of his mother. With all the loss she'd suffered, with the loss she was setting herself up for, she had considered his family's needs. Alex slipped a little in love with Violet. Perhaps it was quick, but he was twenty-five and had never felt anything close to the tenderness she evoked. "Will you recognize him even if he's disguised as Santa?"

She touched her nose. "We share the Yugoslavian *schnoz*. I'll know if he's my father."

7

For Violet, November passed in an odd mix of hot and cold. Alex kept his promises. He showed up most nights when she got off of work, followed her to the house, and walked inside to be sure it was safe before she got out of her car. He chopped wood on Saturday and shoveled her walkways after every snow. He took her out to eat, held her hand during a couple movies, and made it quite clear to everyone at the Mauer's for Thanksgiving that she was his gal.

When he'd walked her to the door that night, he'd rested his forehead on hers and said, "I don't know how you were raised, Violet, but my mother taught me never to date unless I was serious about somebody. Not to keep dating unless she was someone I'd consider marrying."

The words had hung between them while she'd gaped, speechless, and his eyes devoured her mouth.

The days got shorter and colder, but inside she was an inferno.

How incredible that someone she'd met two and a half months before had gone from complete stranger to enemy to the best part of her life. She was so close to being head over heels for him that a different reason for not wanting to meet her father arose.

Alex reported to Fort Riley, Kansas in five weeks. Regardless of their growing attachment, her longing for a father was two decades in the making. How would such a new relationship survive if Santa Dan turned out to be Milo Poplovich?

Scenario one: Her father walked in the door and was innocent of deserting. She'd want to spend every waking moment with him. Alex moved to Fort Riley, and the relationship was over.

Scenario two: Her father was a deserter. Alex would want justice. She couldn't blame him, but she'd not be able to forgive him for sending her father to prison—at least not enough to marry him.

Blood—as the saying went—was thicker than water.

Her imagination flared hotter, leaving her cold with dread.

What if her father was something worse than a deserter? What if he'd not only run but, when confronted, turned on his commanding officer and shot him? Would Alex still love her if her father murdered his?

How could he?

Knowing the scenario was nothing but wild fear didn't help, praying didn't help, nothing helped. And the first Tuesday in December, the last day the volunteers would be meeting to write letters and, therefore, the last day Santa Dan could come thank them, was two days away.

Violet sat in the choir loft fidgeting with the folds of her navy-blue choir robe. Jennifer Mauer nudged her with an elbow and pointed to the top right corner of the hymnal. Startled, Violet grabbed a red hymn book from the wooden pew rack in front of her and turned to the correct page.

She'd missed the entire sermon with her fretting. Red-faced with chagrin, she turned her attention to Pastor Woodhouse and listened to him explain the story behind "It Is Well With My Soul."

Her cares fell away as she listened.

"Horatio G. Spafford was a successful lawyer and businessman in Chicago with a lovely family— a wife, Anna, and five children. However, they were not strangers to tears and tragedy. Their young son died with pneumonia in 1871 and, in that same year, much of their business was lost in the great Chicago fire. Yet, God in His mercy and kindness allowed the business to flourish once more.

"On Nov. 21, 1873, the French ocean liner, Ville du Havre, was crossing the Atlantic from the U.S. to Europe with 313 passengers on board. Among the passengers were Mrs. Spafford and their four daughters. Although Mr. Spafford had planned to go with his family, he found it necessary to stay in Chicago to help solve an unexpected business problem. He told his wife he would join her and their children in Europe a few days later. His plan was to take another ship.

"About four days into the crossing of the Atlantic, the Ville du Harve collided with a powerful, iron-hulled Scottish ship, the Loch Earn. Suddenly, all of those on board were in grave danger. Anna hurriedly brought her four children to the deck. She knelt there with Annie, Margaret Lee, Bessie and Tanetta and prayed that God would spare them if that could be His will, or to make them willing to endure whatever awaited them. Within approximately 12 minutes, the Ville du Harve slipped beneath the dark waters of the Atlantic, carrying with it 226 of the passengers including the four Spafford children.

"A sailor, rowing a small boat over the spot where the ship went down, spotted a woman floating on a piece of the wreckage. It was Anna, still alive. He pulled her into the boat and they were picked up by another large vessel which, nine days later, landed them in Cardiff, Wales. From there she wired her husband a message which began, 'Saved alone, what shall I do?' Mr. Spafford later framed the telegram and placed it in his office.

"Another of the ship's survivors, Pastor Weiss, later recalled Anna saying, 'God gave me four daughters. Now they have been taken from me. Someday I will understand why.'

"Mr. Spafford booked passage on the next available ship and left to join his grieving wife. With the ship about four days out, the captain called

Spafford to his cabin and told him they were over the place where his children went down.

"According to Bertha Spafford Vester, a daughter born after the tragedy, Spafford wrote 'It Is Well With My Soul' while on this journey.

"With the Spafford's story in mind, let us sing this wonderful hymn of faith together."

The organ began to play, but Violet couldn't see the words for the tears blurring her vision. The congregation sang, and her heart caught on the phrase, "Whatever my lot, thou hast taught me to say, 'It is well, it is well with my soul.'"

Taught to say it is well.

Was this the lesson God had for her? To learn how to trust Him in times of peace and when sorrows like sea billows rolled? Or when her imagination spun nightmares?

Somehow, Violet stood through the entire hymn. When the pastor asked everyone to bow their heads for the benediction, she slipped out the choir loft door, ran down the steps to hang up her robe, and was out the door before the organist began the recessional music.

It didn't keep Alex from showing up at her door twenty minutes later. "Hey, beautiful. What's wrong?"

Too wrung out to hide her fears, Violet spilled every last one while they sat at her kitchen table holding hands. She watched him, anxious to read the expressions crossing his face, not sure which she wanted more: for him to find her foolish or to take her seriously.

Either way, she lost.

When she finished talking, Alex scooted his chair until they sat side-by-side. "Remember how I told you my mother was spit on at the grocery store one day?"

How could she forget?

"What I didn't tell you was that her friend was there and was almost arrested for trying to strangle the man. I was ten at the time, and in my 'super spy' phase, complete with toy binoculars."

The image made Violet smile.

"I snuck up and overheard Mrs. Stray ask my mother how she stayed so calm. Mom said, 'Because God gives grace to those who are wronged.' Mrs. Stray got red in the face and stomped out of the house."

"Why?"

"I asked the very same question, even though I knew it meant confessing I'd been spying and would lose my dinner."

Violet squeezed Alex's hand. "Your mother sounds like she knew how to control three rambunctious boys."

"That she did." He smiled at the apparent memory. "She also knew that sometimes it was better to satisfy my curiosity than let me chase down information. After she told me what happened at the store and Mrs. Stray's reaction, Mom said, 'Although I appreciate my friend's loyalty, she's becoming bitter. God gives grace to me, because I am the one being wronged. He doesn't give grace to those who take offense on my behalf.' I remember it word-for-word, because she was taking me to task for my bitterness, too. I imagine the same principle applies to your fears."

"That God gives grace to those who actually go through a tragedy rather than those who conjure up tragedies?"

Alex wrapped an arm around her shoulders. "Exactly."

No wonder she was crazy about the man. He both took her seriously and didn't find her foolish. "Thank you."

He hugged her tighter. "Look Violet, I've run every scenario you spelled out through my head, too, but what good will dwelling on it do? I'll be there on Tuesday. Whatever happens, we'll face it together."

*****

By Tuesday night, Violet had sung "It Is Well With My Soul" a thousand times inside her head and prayed God would teach her how to believe it.

Several of the volunteers offered to bring Christmas cookies to share on their last night of letter writing. Violet decorated with a green table cloth and some hand-cut snowflakes. As the volunteers entered the library basement, Violet took their cookie trays. The table was full by the time Alex and his soldiers arrived.

He came straight to her and put his arm around her waist, his familiar cologne wrapping her in its spell. "You look beautiful tonight."

Violet warmed at his words as well has his touch.

He leaned close to her ear. "Are you ready?"

"Yes and no."

He gave her a squeeze. "We'll get through it together."

The volume of children's letters was the largest yet. After thanking everyone for coming, Violet set them to work. Julie came downstairs to relay a message from Con Miller that Santa would be arriving around eight-thirty.

Another hour of stomach twisting agony.

Alex raised his eyebrows to ask if she was okay.

She nodded and walked to the other side of the room.

At eight-fifteen, jingling bells and a hearty, "Ho, ho, ho!" drifted down the stairs.

Every muscle tensed. She wasn't ready. Not yet.

Alex stood. "Sounds like we're about to have a visit from Santa." He waved his hand, and all the soldiers stood. The rest of the volunteers followed their lead. As they formed a semi-circle around the door, Alex stepped back and drew Violet to the side. "Together, remember?"

Her neck was so tight she couldn't nod. She swallowed and grabbed his hand.

Footsteps thumped on the stairs.

Violet's heart pounded against her sternum.

She saw the beard before she saw the nose.

Not like hers.

Not her father.

And, judging by the look on Alex's face, not his father either.

8

*A*lex pulled Violet into a crushing hug. She pressed her face into his chest to muffle her sobs. A few of the letter writing volunteers looked their way, so Alex turned until she was hidden from view.

Who was this Dan fellow? Santa or no, Alex would pummel the man into mush for making his precious Violet cry.

Alex glanced over his shoulder. Santa was handing out candy canes and thanking each volunteer for making children all over the United States smile. Alex patted Violet's back and whispered assurances until she shuddered to a stop. "You about done crying down there, sweetheart?"

She leaned back and nodded. "I…I think so."

He wiped gray smudges from under her eyes. "You women and makeup. If ever there was a time to *not* wear it…"

Violet snickered and pulled a hanky from her sleeve. Instead of dabbing at her eyes, she wiped at his shirt front. "I'm sorry for blubbering all over you."

Another glance confirmed that Santa was getting closer. "Do you want to meet this guy here or upstairs away from the crowd?"

"Upstairs." Violet took hold of Alex's forearm. "You're coming with me, right?"

He kissed her hair. "Yes, ma'am."

As they made their way to the opposite side of the room, Alex glared at Santa and jerked his head toward the stairs.

A wide grin split Santa's face.

It seemed glares were ineffective on men who weren't subordinates.

Violet started up the stairs. She didn't seem ready to faint, but Alex kept his hand on her back as he followed just in case. Her skirt brushed against his thighs and put images in his mind best left alone.

They made their way to the Alaska Room, a small side chamber where the books were either about the state or by local authors. Outside the window, a curtain of green light swayed in the sky and reflected tiny sparkles in the snow.

"He had a nice smile, don't you think?" Violet wrapped her arms across her waist.

What?

"And Mr. Miller said he was a good man, so there's nothing to worry about, right?"

Alex stepped close and put an arm over her shoulders. "You have nothing to worry about."

Even with the assurance, she tensed when bells jingled, their volume increasing.

His stomach felt like a hundred spinning tops were vying for space inside it. "Would you like to sit down?"

She shook her head and put one arm around his waist. "No."

They turned in unison at a deep, "Hello?" Santa crossed the little room and stuck out his hand, a cheery smile on his lips. "Violet Poplovich, as I live and breathe. I was right sorry to hear about your mother." He shook her hand and turned to Alex. "And you must be Harold Stevens's boy. You're his spitting image."

Alex gripped the extended hand. "You...you know me?"

"Knew your father." Santa took off his hat and wig. "Hope you don't mind. This get-up is hot and scratchy."

Still grappling with this turn of events, Alex looked for a place to sit. Even if Violet didn't need it, he did. There was only one chair in the room. He begged Violet to sit in it with his eyes, then stood behind her gripping the chair back.

Without his fake hair, Santa looked like an ordinary man with white hair and blue eyes. "Dan Christianson, at your service."

The small room could hardly contain the silence.

Dan squinted and looked between Violet and Alex. "What's wrong? You two look like you've seen a ghost."

"And you're acting like I should know you." Alex leaned on the chair.

"I served under your father in Combat Command B."

Violet gasped. "So you knew my father, too?"

"Of course I did." Dan frowned at Violet. "We were best buddies during the war. He asked me to look after you and your ma if anything happened to him. As soon as I got home and settled, I started sending a little every month. I wasn't much, but it was the best I could do."

Alex's heart pounded against his rib cage like horse hooves at a gallop. "Are you the one who replaced her tires and gave her the coat?"

Dan nodded. "When Mr. Mannester down at the bank told me about your mother's death, which—again—I'm awfully sorry to hear about, he mentioned your tires were in bad shape. Told me where I could find you and described your car. My wife added the coat. Thought you might need that, too. I was going to come into the library and introduce myself, but then I heard about President Kennedy's address and rushed home. I left you the card, though. I figured you'd remember me better as the man who sent you letters as Santa when you were a child than as Dan Christianson."

Violet gripped her hands together. "Thank you. It was very kind."

If she wasn't going to mention how frightened the gifts made her, Alex figured he shouldn't either. "How well did you know my father?"

One shoulder lifted. "No better than the rest of us enlisted men, I suppose. Good officer. Well respected for his knowledge and fair treatment of his men. A shame to lose him."

"What…what happened to them? Our fathers?" Violet's knuckles were white.

Alex put a hand on her shoulder. "All we know is they were accused of desertion."

Dan's eyes went wide. "What!"

An older gentleman sitting five feet away turned a scathing glance toward them.

Dan opened the two buttons closest to his neck. "Those nitwits. If I ran my business the way they run the army, we'd be sunk."

Alex felt Violet's muscles tremble under his hand. He squeezed her shoulder. "What do you mean?"

Dan continued to unbutton his Santa top, revealing a white T-shirt underneath. "You've no doubt heard of the Battle of Bastogne."

Alex and Violet nodded.

"Miserable business." Dan took off the Santa top and folded it. "Most scared I've ever been in my life, and I don't mind saying so. Scared all of us, truth be told, but Poplovich had it worse than any of us."

Alex opened his mouth to ask why, but shut it at the look Dan sent him.

"When it came time for our next mission, Milo balked. Said he couldn't force himself inside a tank. Not again. I told him to go someplace to clear his head because there was no way the Old Man— that's what we called General Patton—would stand for one of his boys failing to do his duty. After about three hours, I went looking for Milo. Figured he'd stay inside the perimeter, but I couldn't find him. I ventured as far as was safe, went back to camp to report him missing to our captain, your father,"—he nodded to Alex—"and we both went out searching."

"I knew it." Seventeen years of tension uncoiled from Alex's bones.

"Did you find him? My father?" Violet's sweet voice trembled.

Dan scratched his ear. "Eventually. But not before he'd been shot."

Alex sat on the floor beside Violet and took her hand, his sixth sense raising hairs on his arms. "What happened after you found him?"

"Stood up, like an idiot, and got myself shot through the stomach. As I was fading to black, I saw two…" Dan bit off his next word. He swallowed and started over. "A Nazi shot the captain, but not before he got off a round that killed the other guy."

Pieces started to come together for Alex. "Were you taken prisoner?"

Dan nodded, his skin tone fading. "All three of us."

"How long?"

"Six months. Your fathers died in that hole. By the time all us POW's were rescued, I was defending myself against a desertion charge."

"But why desertion when there were so many who went missing who were never charged?" Alex felt ready to burst now he was hearing the truth.

"Based off what they asked me, I'd say I wasn't the only one that heard Milo talk about running off. As for the captain, there was a lieutenant we all hated who might've made trouble. Anyway, I figured since they cleared me, they must've cleared Milo and the captain, too. Guess I figured wrong." Dan pounded a fist into his palm. "The nitwits."

Violet straightened slowly. "My father, too?"

Dan's blue eyes crinkled. "After I woke up and was well enough to go see Milo, he said, 'I was coming back, Danny-boy. I promise. I was coming back.'"

Violet turned shining eyes on Alex. "Did you hear, Alex? My father didn't desert either."

Not caring that it was entirely inappropriate in a library, Alex swiveled onto his knees and kissed Violet Poplovich with seventeen years worth of past due celebration.

*****

Alex and Violet flew to Kansas City on Christmas Eve, their present to his mother tucked inside her purse.

Violet wasn't sure which made her more nervous, flying or meeting Alex's mother.

"Don't worry, she'll love you." Alex took her hand.

"And if she doesn't?"

He poked the purse clutched in her lap with his pinkie. "That's why *you're* giving her Mr. Christianson's letter."

Even though Dan had written out what he told them in the library, Violet knew it might not be enough to clear her father. But it didn't matter what the army ruled. Her father had been a hero, and her mother…well…she'd never fully understand what her mother had been thinking. Had she intended to tell the truth as she knew it at some point? Was that why she kept the Santa letters and deposit slips together? She'd taken the checks, written to Dan to ask him to send Violet letters, but never asked about the desertion charge. Perhaps Mom knew her husband wasn't a deserter in her heart, or perhaps she feared hearing he was.

After the past few months, Violet understood why it might have been easier to cling to what she wanted to be true rather than risk hearing the opposite.

Mr. Christianson's letter explaining about the imprisonment would clear Alex's father, though the news might not be enough to garner Mrs. Stevens's blessing so Violet could wear the ring Alex had tucked in his pocket. The daughter of an army deserter might not be a good wife for a rising officer like Alex.

Either way, Lord, teach me to say it is well with my soul.

Alex's brother, David, was waiting for them when the stepped off the plane. A slightly shorter and equally handsome version of his brother, David picked Violet up and swung her in a circle. "So you're the legendary Violet Poplovich. Nice to meet you."

She blushed to her roots. "Nice to meet you, too."

Alex grabbed his brother and gave him a pounding hug. "Scoundrel. Stop trying to steal my girl."

David winked at Violet. "Can't blame a guy for trying."

Charmed and somewhat eased by his warm reception, she hung back and let David and Alex catch up while they collected baggage and drove through the streets of Kansas City.

As they pulled into Alex's neighborhood, he rolled down the windows to let in the sound of Christmas carolers roaming from door to door.

"All is calm, all is bright…"

They turned into a driveway, and Violet's spirit was neither calm nor bright.

Either way, Lord. Either way.

Alex opened the car door and helped her out. "Together, remember?"

Violet nodded. "But I won't go against her wishes. I've lost my mother. I won't be the cause of you losing yours."

The usual, *"Don't worry,"* didn't come from Alex's lips.

The knot in her stomach cinched tighter.

David opened the front door of the one-story rambler with a flourish. "Hey, Mom. I've brought you a Christmas present. Two of them, actually."

"David Andrew Stevens, what are you up to?" The feminine voice and the use of three names meant it could only be Alex's mother. "We're going to be late for the candlelight service."

Alex stepped through the door, pulling Violet into the cookie-scented living room decorated with a tree, presents, four stockings, and a "Merry Christmas" banner strung over the fireplace mirror.

A tall, thin woman turned from the dining room alcove and shrieked. "Alex!"

He let go of Violet and ran to meet his mother, whirling her in a circle.

The whirling greeting was obviously as much a part of the family as their tall, dark, and handsome looks.

"I didn't know you were coming. Oh…this is just the best Christmas present ever." She patted Alex's cheek and beamed up at him.

"I think you'll like this present just as much." Alex wrapped an arm around his mother and led her to Violet. "Mom, I'd like you to meet the woman I've been searching for all my life, Violet Poplovich."

Violet blushed and put out her right hand. "It's a pleasure to meet you, Mrs. Stevens."

Alex's mom by-passed the handshake, and pulled Violet into a warm hug. "Welcome to our home, Miss Poplovich."

Either way, Lord. Either way.

She opened her purse and pulled out an envelope. "For you, Mrs. Stevens. It's a letter from Santa.".

ABOUT THE AUTHOR

Becca Whitham (WIT-um) is a multi-published author who has always loved reading and writing stories. After raising two children, she and her husband faced the empty nest years by following their dreams: he joined the army as a chaplain, and she began her journey toward publication. Becca loves to tell stories marrying real historical events with modern-day applications to inspire readers to live Christ-reflecting lives. She's traveled to almost every state in the U.S. for speaking and singing engagements and has lived in Washington, Oregon, Colorado, Oklahoma, and Alaska.

www.beccawhitham.com
becca-expressions.blogspot.com

Other books by Becca Whitham

Made in the USA
Charleston, SC
25 November 2015